Come on, Daisy

Jane Simmons

ORCHARD BOOKS

To my Mum

ORCHARD BOOKS
96 Leonard Street, London EC2A 4XD
Hachette Children's Books
Level 17/207 Kent Street, Sydney, NSW 2000
First published in Great Britain in 1998
This edition published for Bookstart in 2005
ISBN 1 84616 097 9
Text and illustrations © Jane Simmons 1998
The right of Jane Simmons to be identified as the author
and illustrator of this work has been asserted by her in
accordance with the Copyright, Designs and Patents Act, 1988.
A CIP catalogue record for this book is available from the British Library.
1 3 5 7 9 10 8 6 4 2
Printed in Singapore

"You must stay close, Daisy,"
said Mamma Duck.
"I'll try," said Daisy.

But Daisy didn't.
"Come on, Daisy!"
called Mamma Duck.

But Daisy was watching the fish.

"Come on, Daisy!" shouted
Mamma Duck again.
But Daisy was far away
chasing dragonflies.

"Come here, Daisy!" shouted Mamma Duck.
But Daisy was bouncing on the lily pads.
Bouncy, bouncy, bouncy.
Bong, bong!

"Plop!" went a frog.
"Coo..." said Daisy.
"Gribbit," said the frog.

Bong, plop!

Bong, plop!

"Coo!" said Daisy, but the
frog had gone.
   "Mamma," called Daisy, but
Mamma Duck had gone.
   Daisy was all alone.

Something big stirred underneath her.
Daisy shivered.

She scrambled up on to the riverbank.
Then something screeched in
the sky above!

So Daisy hid in the reeds.
If only Mamma Duck was here.

Something was
rustling along the
riverbank.
    Daisy could hear
it getting closer...

...and closer,
and closer,
and...
CLOSER...

It was Mamma!
"Daisy, come on!" she said.
And Daisy did.

And even though she played
with the butterflies...

she stayed very close to Mamma Duck.